D0014387

The Little Mermaid

Retold by Katie Daynes

Illustrated by
Alan Marks

Reading consultant: Alison Kelly
Roehampton University

Contents

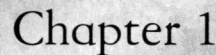

Chapter 1

The deep blue sea

Far out at sea,
     below the waves,
     deeper
     and deeper
          and deeper still,
     stood the
     Sea King's castle.

There, at the very bottom of the sea, the water was as clear as glass. The sand was as fine as powder. Tall seaweed grew up around the castle walls and small, bright fish darted among its branches.

The Sea King was very proud of his castle. It was the perfect place to bring up his six mermaid daughters.

Each daughter
was given her own
small garden to care for.
"I'm going to shape mine
like a whale," said the eldest.

"Mine will
have a seashell
border," said
the next.

"And I'm
going to grow
pretty flowers,"
said the third.

The fourth and fifth mermaids loved exploring. "Let's decorate our gardens with treasure from shipwrecks," they said.

Then their little sister appeared, hugging a statue of a smiling boy. "Look what I've found!" she cried. "I'm going to put *him* in my garden."

7

The sisters spent all day in the castle waters, tending their gardens and playing games. In the evening, as the sea turned to inky black, their grandmother called them inside for supper.

Lying on silky cushions, the family ate steaming seaweed parcels and soft sea fruits.

"Tell us a story, Grandmama," begged the littlest mermaid.

Grandmama had seen the world above the waves. She told amazing tales of men with two legs and no tail.

"There are buildings as tall as the ocean is deep," she said, "and machines that glide even faster than sharks."

The little mermaid hung on her every word.

"When you reach fifteen," announced the Sea King, "you may rise above the waves and see these things for yourselves."

While the older sisters flicked their tails in delight, the little mermaid sat drumming her fingers. "That's six whole years away!" she sighed.

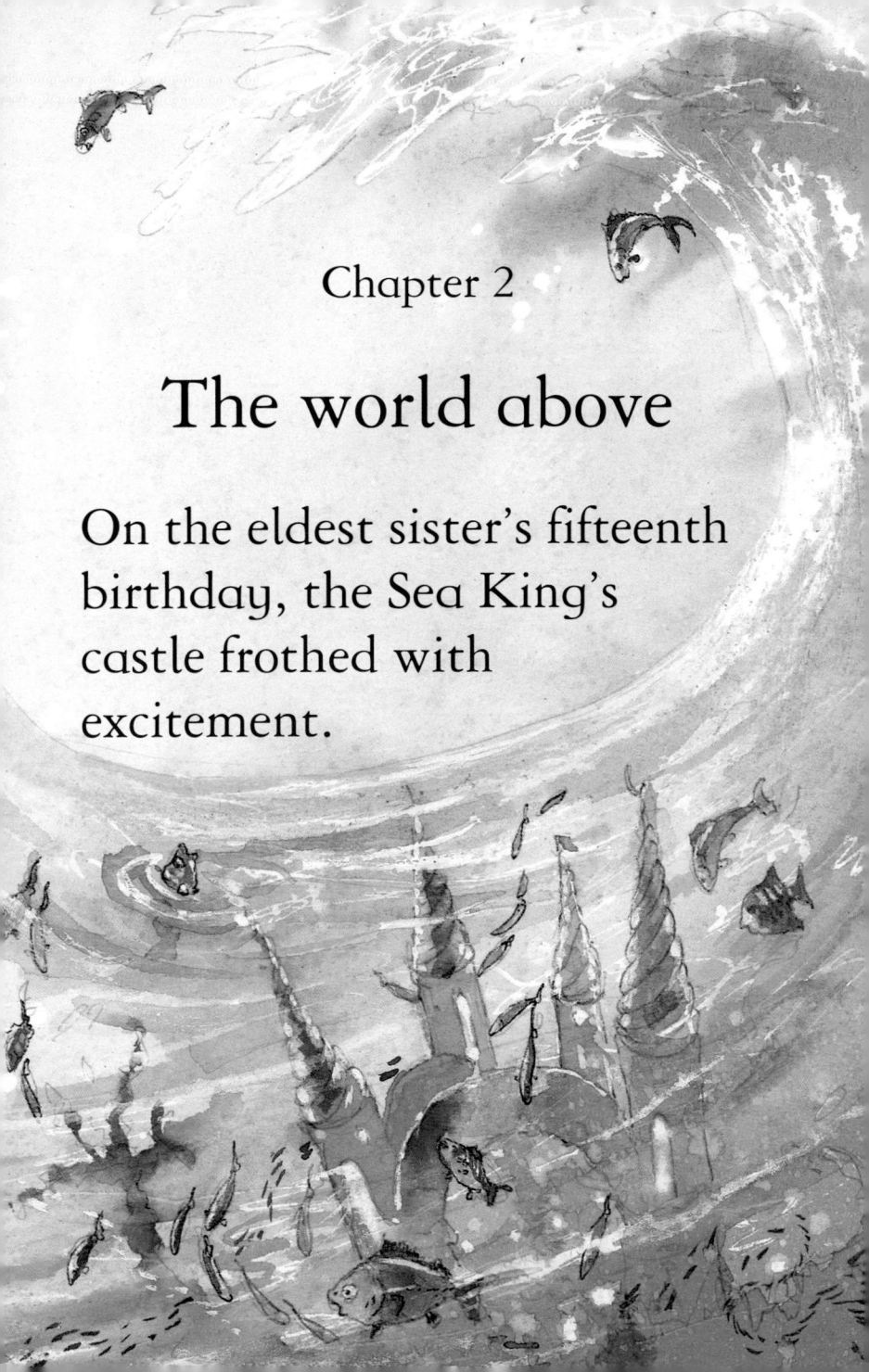

Chapter 2

The world above

On the eldest sister's fifteenth birthday, the Sea King's castle frothed with excitement.

The mermaids showered
their big sister with twinkling
pearls. But the best present of
all was the Sea King's blessing.
"Now you can swim to the
surface of the sea," he said.

12

"Come back quickly!" called the little mermaid. She wanted to hear *everything* about the world above.

Her sister finally returned, grinning with excitement. "I watched the sun sink into the sea," she said. "Its orange light flooded the water."

Ooooh!

For hours, the mermaids pestered her with questions.

Did you see land?

Were there any boats?

What does air feel like?

Her littlest sister was the most curious. "Did the wind stroke your hair?" she asked. "Did the sun kiss your cheeks?"

14

That night, the little
mermaid gazed at the sea
above. A black blot glided
through the water.

"It must be a ship!" she
thought. "I wonder who's on
it and where they're going..."
She fell asleep and dreamed
of sailing the ocean.

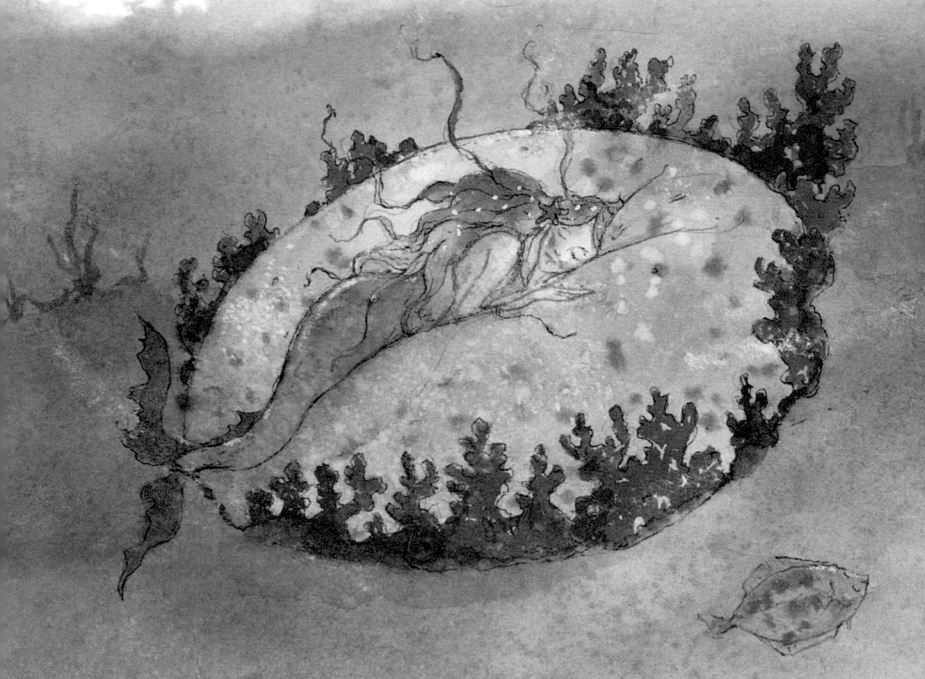

Chapter 3

Rescue from the storm

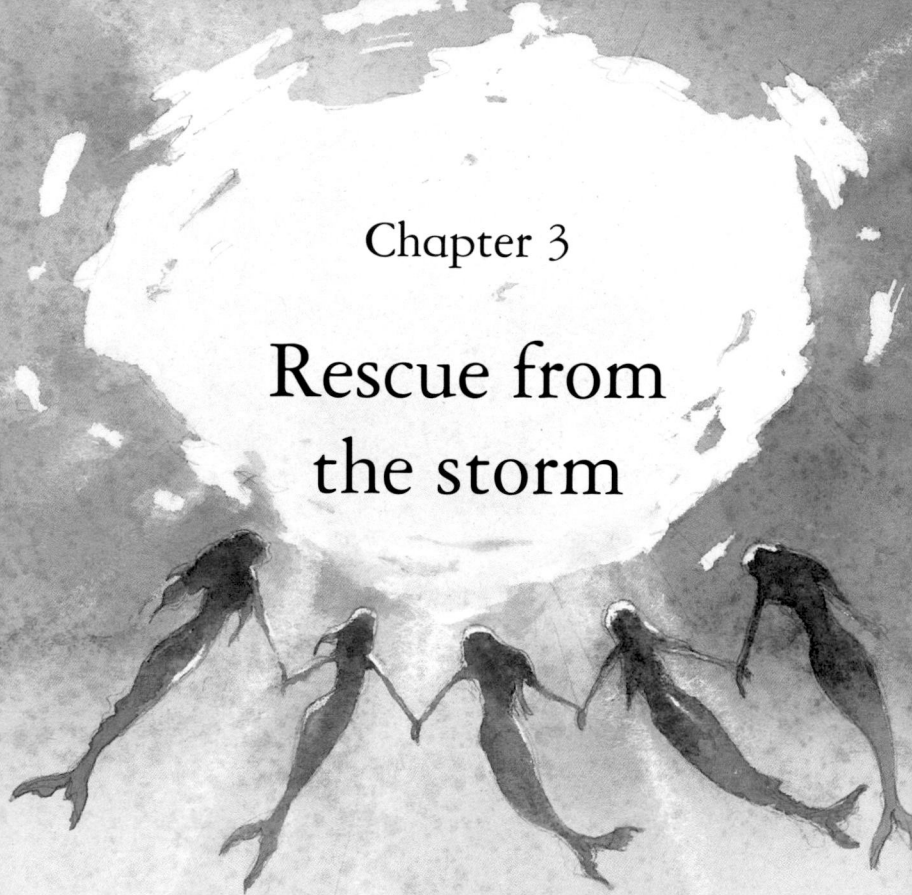

One by one, the sisters reached fifteen and were allowed to swim above the waves. The little mermaid watched them rise up, hand in hand, longing for the day she could join them.

16

As time dragged on, the little mermaid spent hours with her statue. "I can't wait to see what dry land looks like," she told him.

Finally, the year... then the month... then the day of her fifteenth birthday arrived. As soon as the celebrations were over, she set off for the surface.

"Goodbye!" she called to her sisters, rising up like a bubble of air. With each swish of her tail, the water felt lighter.

Her head broke through the waves and she gasped. The sun was setting, just as her sister had described. And there, ahead, floated a ship.

18

The little mermaid swam
closer. Lanterns hung from the
masts and lively music filled
the air. Closer still, she saw
people dancing on deck.

She stared in delight as their two legs carried them back and forth. A handsome young man appeared, wearing a crown.

"Happy birthday, Prince Milo!" the people shouted, as a hundred rockets exploded in the sky.

The little mermaid watched the prince, enchanted. It was as if her statue had come to life.

Suddenly, the weather turned stormy and everyone ran below deck. Waves rose up like mountains around the creaking ship and a streak of lightning split the dark clouds.

21

The little mermaid rode the surf with glee, but then she heard cries from the ship. The wind and waves were battering it apart, tossing terrified people into the foaming sea.

The mermaid was horrified. "They'll never survive without tails," she thought. "Oh, the poor prince. I must find him..."

She searched everywhere, diving between beams and planks.

At last she saw him, clinging to a broken mast.

She pulled the prince to a sheltered cove and let the waves wash him ashore.

"Thank you," he murmured.

The little mermaid watched from a clump of seaweed. As the dawn light warmed the sky, a pretty girl came and helped the prince to his feet. Smiling, he looked out to sea, then walked away.

Chapter 4

Finding
her prince

The little mermaid floated
joyfully back to the castle.

"How was it?" her sisters
asked together.

"Beautiful," she sighed.

All day, the sisters played in the castle waters.

"Catch!" cried the eldest, throwing a sponge ball.

But the little mermaid was too busy dreaming of walking with her prince.

That night, and every night for a week, she swam back to the cove and gazed longingly at the empty beach.

At dawn, she returned to her statue under the sea. "Will I ever see my prince again?" she asked. The marble boy just smiled.

"Why do you swim to the same place each night?" asked her sisters, one morning.

The little mermaid blushed and told them about her prince.

"I've seen that prince," said the eldest sister. "He lives in a grand palace by the sea."

"Really?" cried the excited little mermaid. "Show me!"

That evening, all six mermaids rose up through the sea and swam to the palace.

It stood proud and shiny at the water's edge. As the mermaids watched, a man strode onto the balcony.

"It's my prince!" cried the little mermaid. "Do you think he's looking for me?"

"Don't be silly," said the eldest sister.

Day after day, the little mermaid returned to the palace. Each time, she swam a little closer.

When the prince went sailing, she swam behind him. She prayed for a storm, so she could save him again. But it never came.

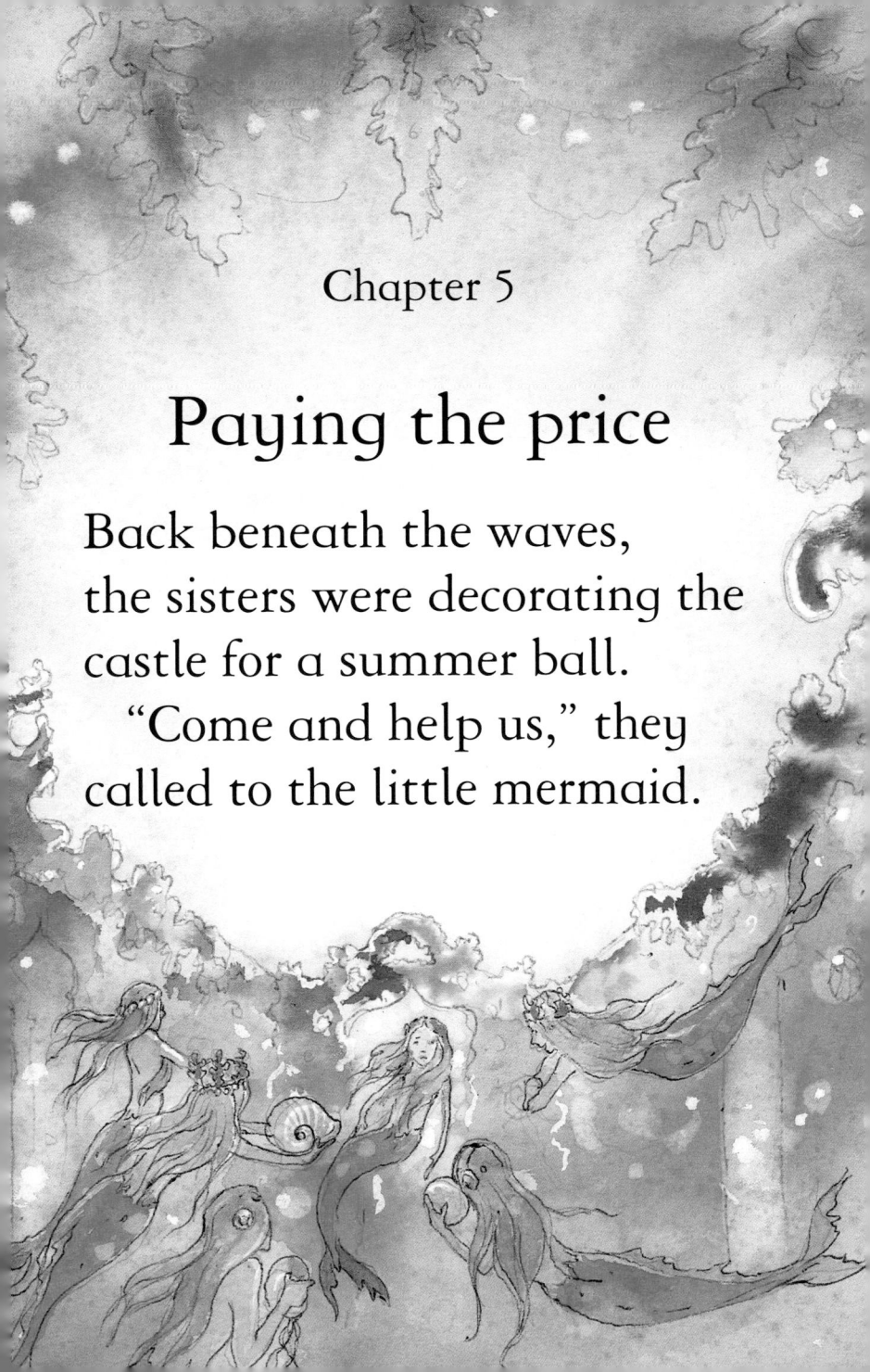

Chapter 5

Paying the price

Back beneath the waves, the sisters were decorating the castle for a summer ball.

"Come and help us," they called to the little mermaid.

She tried to tie ribbons, but she just couldn't concentrate.

"You're not *still* thinking about that prince, are you?" said her eldest sister.

The little mermaid nodded.

"Remember, he's a man and you're a mermaid," her sister went on. "He will only make you unhappy."

By nightfall, the sea castle
looked splendid. Blue flames
rose up from pearly white
shells, lighting the way
from the gardens to
the hall.

Guests streamed
in, wearing
shimmery clothes...

...and a fish
band sang
gurgling tunes.

33

The little mermaid pretended to join in, but she couldn't stop thinking of her prince. "I have to do something," she thought. "Maybe the sea witch can help me..."

While her sisters swayed to the fish band's songs, the little mermaid swam away.

It was a dark and dangerous journey to the sea witch's cave. The little mermaid crossed bubbling hot mud...

dodged swirling whirlpools...

...and darted past slimy seaweed arms.

35

At last, the craggy cave loomed up ahead. The ugly sea witch stood at the entrance.

"So you want legs to impress a prince," she snapped. (The sea witch knew everything.) "They will cost you dearly."

"But I have nothing to give you," said the little mermaid.

36

"Yes you do," the witch declared. "Your voice."

The little mermaid gulped. "But how will I talk to my prince?" she asked.

"That's not my problem."

The witch started stirring a potion. "This will split your tail in two," she said, "and give you human legs."

"But there are two things you should know," she added. "One, if you drink this potion, you can never go back to your father's castle. And two, if the prince doesn't return your love... you will dissolve into the ocean waves."

The witch stopped stirring and looked up. "Do you still want to drink it?" she asked.

The little mermaid didn't pause. "I do," she replied. They were the last words she ever spoke.

With a wave of her wand, the witch added the mermaid's voice to her potion.

Chapter 6

The prince's bride

By dawn, the little mermaid was sitting on a sea rock near the palace. In her trembling hand she held a bottle of the witch's potion.

Suddenly, a door opened
and the prince stepped onto
his balcony. He stretched,
yawned and gazed out to sea.

The sight of the prince made
the mermaid bolder. She
swallowed the potion, jumped
into the water... spluttered,
splashed and nearly drowned.
Her tail had split into legs.

The prince saw the splashes. "Who's that?" he called. "Somebody help her."

A servant waded in and pulled the little mermaid to safety. Soon she was standing in front of her prince.

"Who are you?" he asked.

She couldn't answer. He asked again. She still couldn't answer. Instead, she smiled.

The prince smiled back.
"Find this young lady some
clothes," he said to his servant.
"She's joining me for breakfast."

The little mermaid spent the
whole day with the prince.
She was very happy but kept
wobbling on her new feet.
"Take my arm," said the
prince. "I'll show you around."

That evening, the little
mermaid stood on the prince's
balcony. Frothy waves danced
on the rocks below. Five
tails flipped by and she
recognized her sisters.

"Come back!" they cried.
The little mermaid
smiled but shook her head.
She had made her choice.

"I don't even know your name," the prince was saying. "But when I saw you in the water this morning, I thought of my own true love."

The mermaid's eyes sparkled and her heart beat faster.

"I almost drowned once," he went on. "I was swept to a beach and woken by a lovely princess. Tomorrow I'm going to set sail and marry her!"

The prince's words were like a dagger in the mermaid's heart. He was everything to her, but he loved someone else.

"Don't worry," he said. "You can come with me."

But the little mermaid shook her head, sobbing silently.

Next morning, she watched her prince sail into the distance.

The world she loved was lost to her. "You can never go back," said the witch's voice inside her head.

"Come to us," sang the ocean spray.

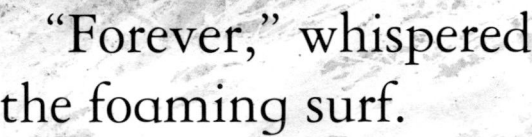

"Forever," whispered the foaming surf.

With tears streaming down her cheeks, the brave little mermaid disappeared into the welcoming waves.

The Little Mermaid was first told by Hans Christian Andersen. He was born in Denmark in 1805. In the town of Copenhagen, where Andersen worked and studied, there's a statue of the little mermaid. She sits on a rock and looks over the water, thinking of her prince.

Series editor: Lesley Sims

Designed by Katarina Dragoslavic

Cover design by Russell Punter

First published in 2005 by Usborne Publishing Ltd., Usborne House, 83-85 Saffron Hill, London EC1N 8RT, England. www.usborne.com
Copyright © 2005 Usborne Publishing Ltd.

48